IT'S VERY KIND OF...

OH, THANK YOU VERY MUCH!

I HOPE A HELPING OF "CAT RICE" IS ENOUGH FOR NOW.

I KNOW THIS ISN'T MUCH, BUT...

HUH? OF COURSE WE DON'T...

It's only a fish and a chicken.

BUT I THOUGHT HUMANKIND DON'T EAT CAT!

WAIT!! DID YOU SAY "CAT RICE"?!

A real cat MEAT?!

ARE YOU GOING TO EAT ME TOO?!

"Cat Rice" refers to the portion size which is similar in size to what the Javanese would serve to a pet cat.

MUNCH MUNCH

AAAAAH

LET'S EAT!

AS THEY'RE PARTS OF US DIVINE BEINGS, WE'RE EXPECTED TO TAKE CARE OF THEM OURSELVES

YOU SEE, OUR MAGICAL CLOTHES POSSESS OUR POWERS INDIVIDUALLY

ARE YOU EXPECTING THEM TO COME BACK AND BRING YOU A SPARE?

NAH, THERE'S NO SUCH THING AS "SPARES" IN KAHYANGAN

No way

WAVE WAVE

IT WILL BE HARD FOR HIM TO SURVIVE AND LIVE HERE BY HIMSELF, THAT'S FOR SURE...

MAYBE THIS IS MY PUNISHMENT FROM DEWATA FOR BEING NEGLIGENT

Tohohohoho

I SEE...

BASICALLY, IN HIS CURRENT CONDITION WITHOUT HIS CLOTHES, HE'S POWERLESS...

HUH?

WHAT IF YOU STAY WITH ME FOR A WHILE?

SAY, LORD GAHAR!

GOSHDARNIT! YOU'RE RIGHT!! THAT'S SUPPOSED TO BE THE FIRST PROBLEM I SHOULD THINK ABOUT!

BUT DON'T YOU THINK WE NEED TO DO SOMETHING ABOUT MY FACE AND APPEARANCE FIRST?

SLAP

OH YEAH, THAT WOULD BE HELPFUL!

SURE YOU DON'T MIND?

I'LL BE GLAD TO!

IN THAT CASE, I'M WILLING TO SHOW YOU THE ROPE

I MEAN, YOU MIGHT NEED TO LEARN HOW HUMANKIND LIVE

Hunting, socializing, working, etc...

A BOO!

FLIP

WHOAH?!

LOOK! LOOK!

PEEEEEEK

?

JAKA! JAKA!

PEOPLE WOULD MISTAKE YOU AS A DEMON!

What am I supposed to do?

CAN YOU DO SOMETHING ELSE OTHER THAN THAT, THOUGH?

NOT WITHOUT MY CLOTHES!

AWWH...

DO YOU THINK I'M SOME KIND OF MAGICIAN?!

I MEAN, GAHAR!

Man, it feels awkward!

I UNDERSTAND, LORD GAHAR!

OI!

SO YOU CAN JUST DROP THE HONORIFICS!

ASIDE OF THAT, I'M NOT DIFFERENT WITH HUMAN!

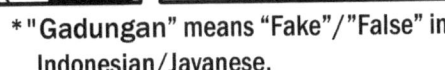

* "Gadungan" means "Fake"/"False" in Indonesian/Javanese.

IT'S DEWATA BASIC STYLE "GADUNGAN ART"!

Now the problems are solved!

THAT WAS AMAZING!

FLUUUSH

Splash Splash

COCK-A-DOODLE-DO

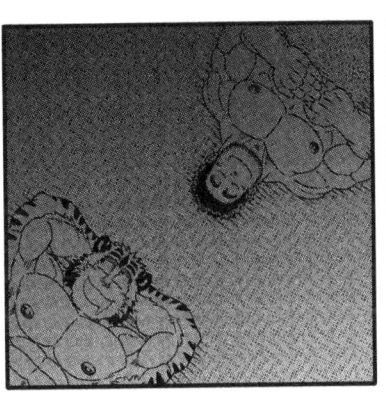

MMMMMMMH

SO, WHAT ARE WE GOING TO DO TODAY?

WELL...

I'M GLAD YOU'RE ENJOYING IT

REALLY!

HUMAN LIFE IS NOT AS BAD AS I THOUGHT!

YOU'LL SEE

HOO, AND WHERE IS IT, EXACTLY?

WE'RE GOING TO GO SOMEWHERE FOR REFRESHING INSTEAD

WE'RE ACTUALLY TAKING A DAY OFF TODAY!

OH?

ZAAAAAASH

YOU'RE WEL-COME!

THIS! IS! HEAVEN!!

AND HERE WE ARE!

WHOAAAH!!

DON'T WORRY! NOBODY WILL COME!

HURRY, JAK! LET'S HAVE A BATH BEFORE SOMEONE ELSE COMES!

WHEN I WANT TO SOOTHE MY MIND, I ALWAYS GO TO THIS PLACE!

IT'S BEEN LIKE, MY PRIVATE SPOT FOR YEARS

NOBODY KNOWS ABOUT THIS PLACE!

HUH?

HOLD

HUH?

LET ME PUT MY CLOTH SOME-WHERE FIRST!

ANYWAY, DON'T MIND ME!

JAKA...

WHEN I HEAR ABOUT YOUR STORY, I CAN'T HELP BUT THINKING "LORD GAHAR WOULD LOVE THIS PLACE"

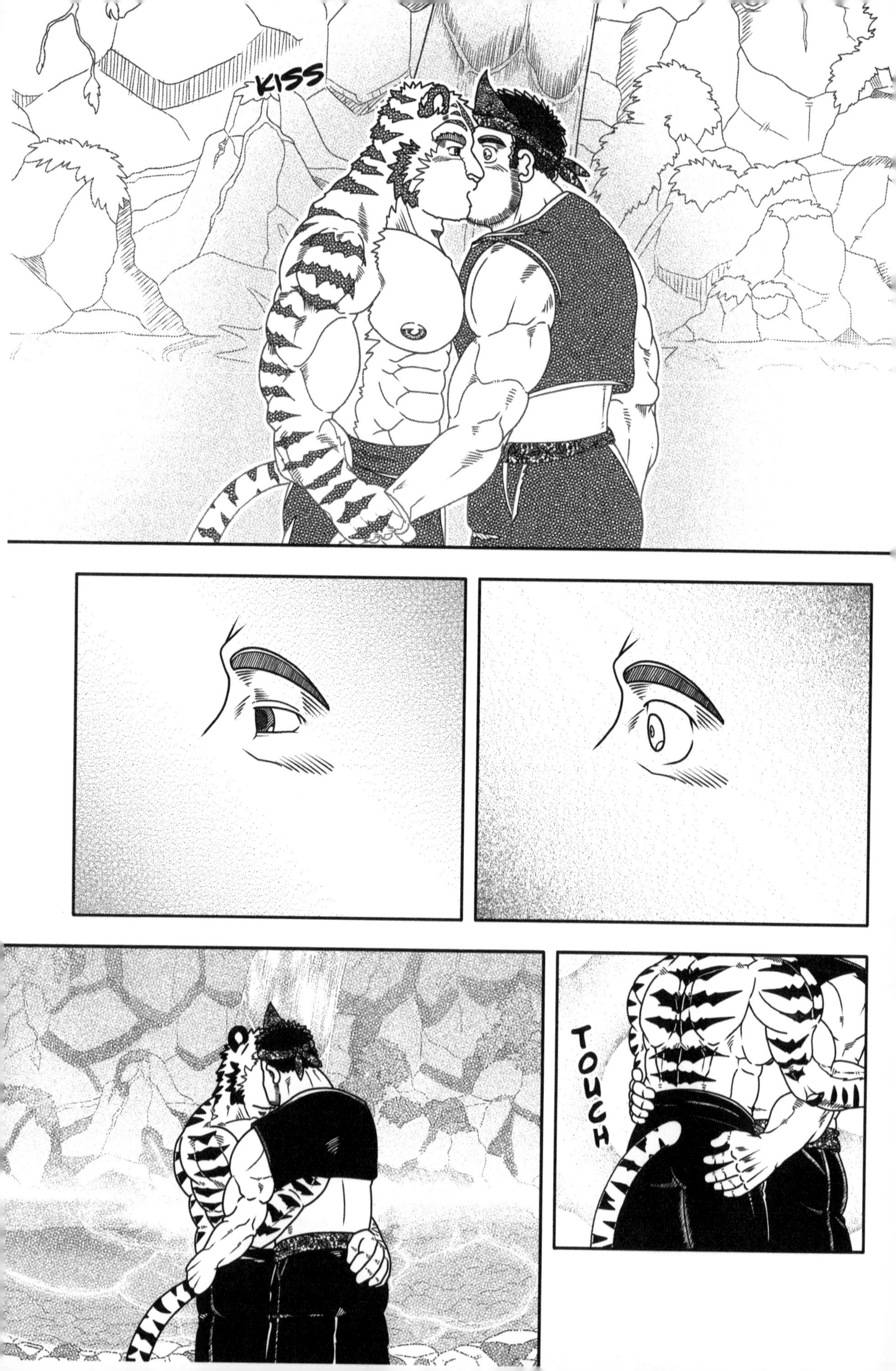

KISS

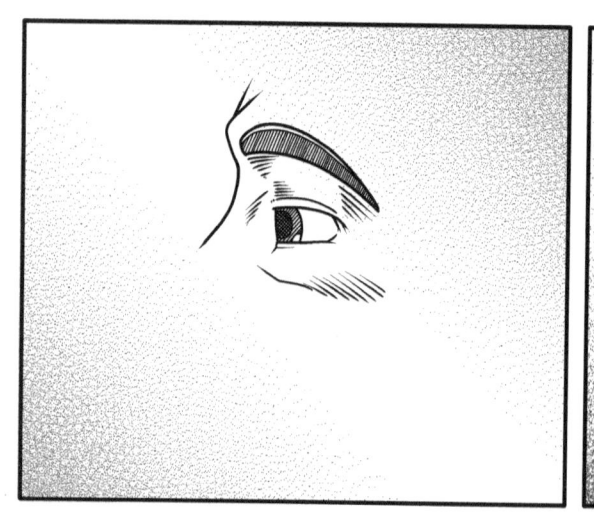

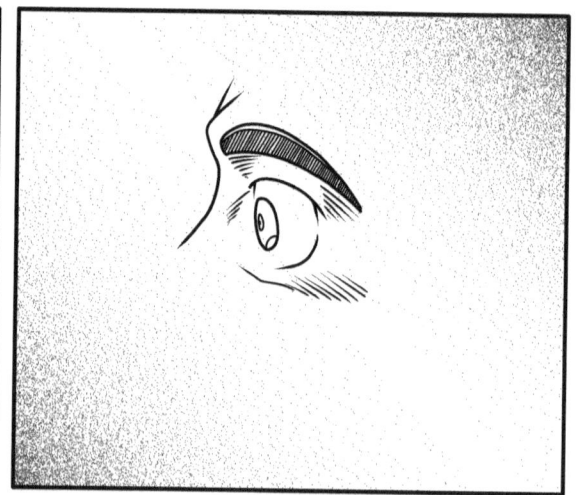

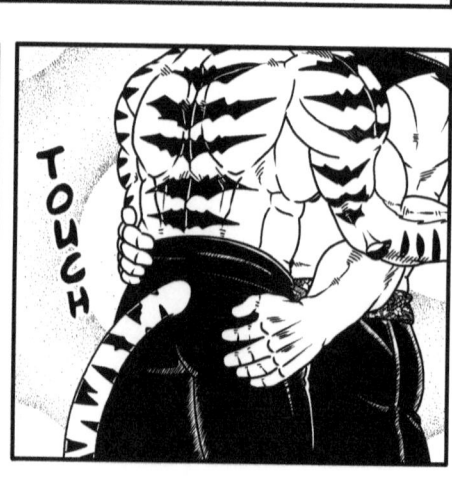

TOUCH

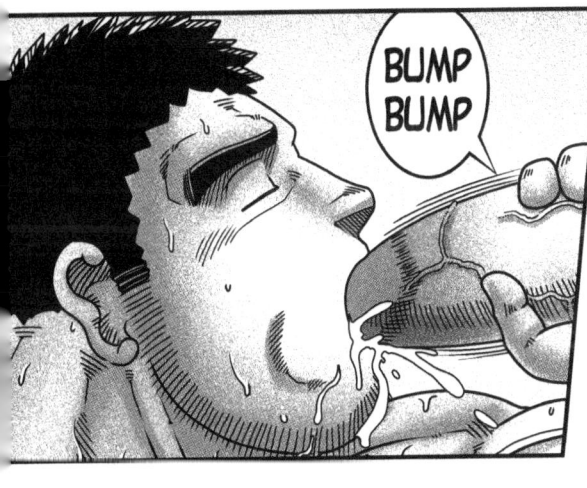

FEW WEEKS LATER...

ALRIGHT! WE'RE GOING TO HUNT BOARS TODAY! ARE YOU READY?

I'M READY!

YOUR BOW?

CHECK!

YOUR ARROW?

CHECK!

GREAT! YOUR AIM IS GETTING BETTER, SO WHAT IF WE GET AT LEAST THREE OF THEM?

LEAVE'EM TO ME, JAK!

AH!

LET ME TAKE IT FOR YOU!

I THINK I SAW IT SOME-WHERE INSIDE THE HOUSE!

THANKS, SORRY TO BOTHER YOU!

RIGHT! WE CAN'T LET OURSELVES THIRSTY!

THE WATER JUG!

YEP, I ALMOST FORGET SOME-THING!

OH, THE ONE FOR DRINKING, RIGHT?

GAHAR SURE IS TAKING HIS TIME...

GAHAR, YOU THERE?

HAVE YOU FOUND THE WATER JUG?

...THESE?

WHAT ARE...

JAKA...

TO BE CONTINUED

www.ingramcontent.com/pod-product-compliance
Lightning Source LLC
Chambersburg PA
CBHW041531120626
46551CB00018B/2652